KUNGSHALL

# THE LABYRINTH

Simon Stålenhag

SIMON &
SCHUSTER

London • New York • Toronto • Sydney • New Delhi

At last I stand near the mountain of the fates.
All around like stormclouds
crowd formless beings, creatures of the twilight,
black-winged,
phosphorous-eyed.
Shall I stay? Shall I go? The road lies dark.
If I stay peacefully here at the foot of the mountain,
then no one will touch me.
[…]

Karin Boye, WALPURGIS NIGHT, 1935.

## THE BLACK GLOBES

*It was first thought to be some kind of cosmic phenomenon. As if our solar system had drifted into an unknown part of the galaxy where there were processes as yet unmapped by human science. The black globes appeared to follow rules and regularities that transcended those of nature or chance. Occasionally, they were seen moving in formation, patiently gliding through the landscape from one place to another.*

*As if they were following a plan of action.*

One summer when we were young, I caught a small snake. I carried it around in a clear plastic container where I had placed some stones and a few fern leaves. When I opened the container to show Matt the snake, he promptly reached his hand in, grabbed the snake and ran away. But he hadn't gone further than a few meters when he gave a panicked scream. The snake had broken in the middle. The front part with the head disappeared under the house and the back part stayed writhing in a small bloody pool in my big brother's palm. Repulsed, he tossed it aside.

I later learned that it hadn't been a snake at all but a slow-worm, a creature that lacks legs and that has the ability to shed its tail. It is a defense mechanism. It is called autotomy. The slow-worm couldn't compete with my brother's intelligence or strength but it could save its life by doing something completely unexpected and unthinkable: perform an act of violence against itself and mutilate its own body.

That was how it managed to escape.

Tomorrow the punishment will be meted out. The chord that is wrapped around my neck will have been boiled in order to minimize any potential elasticity and the part that forms the noose will be smeared with paraffin. It will be a large ceremony with many participants. Everyone will see it. The public part of the punishment has great significance. Deterrence has always been an important part of this project. I understand that they don't believe my story. I mean, his head is severed. And I'm assuming they saw the symbol on the knife.

As far as guilt is concerned, I am brimming with it. Honestly speaking, I don't think it matters very much anymore. I can hardly understand what happened myself. The past few weeks have blurred together in my head. When did things start to go wrong?

I am so tired. Let me think back.

Yes, Charlie.

Charlie was a child who acted out.

The Kungshall school system doesn't have the resources for such a child. I can understand that.

He was happy not to have to go to school for a while. And in addition, we were going to get to see the Earth's surface. We viewed it as a little adventure. A break from the daily routine at Kungshall would do him good. The negative pattern that had emerged at school would be interrupted. The psychologist agreed with us about this. So we took him along to Granhammar.

You have to keep in mind that we have done this for seven years now. These expeditions are routine. You go to one of the stations up there: Vendelsberg, Ånäs, Bergudden. Or Granhammar. You live there for a few weeks, go on excursions, obtain samples, measure the temperature and air pressure, take pictures, service the measuring equipment.

During the forty-five expeditions that have been dispatched from Kungshall since the beginning of the project, we have only had one death – and that was entirely due to the human factor. It was a geologist who, during a surface excursion, had an epileptic seizure, fell and crushed his helmet visor. But he had kept his epilepsy secret so as not to lose his place at Kungshall. We would never have deliberately let anyone through with such a serious illness.

So if we disregard geologists who keep serious health conditions secret, the statistics looked very good. And, for heaven's sake, it wasn't as if we were planning to take the boy on a walk on the surface: he was going to watch movies and play games at Granhammar for a week.

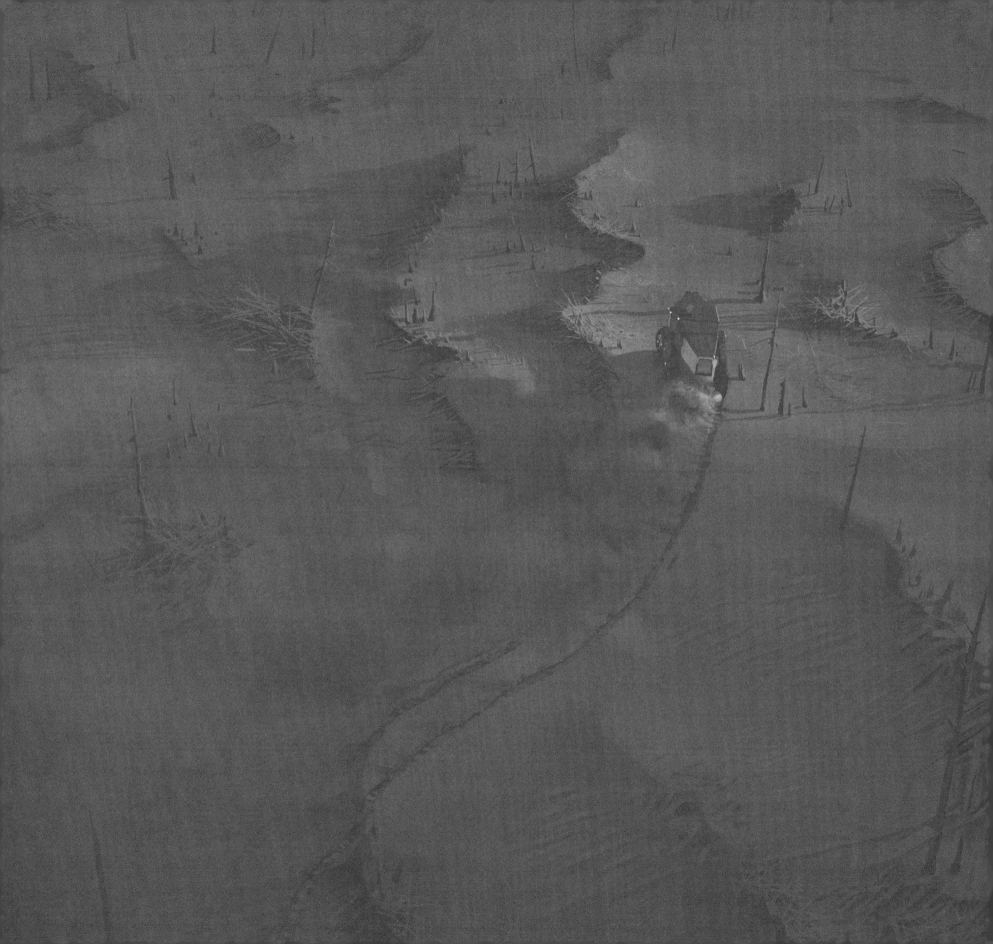

The entire way to the station, Matt sat in the lookout with Charlie. He tried to think of things to tell the boy about the world outside the all-terrain vehicle. When the sun appeared before us on the motorway, he told Charlie that the sun is actually not green and that it is the ammonia in the atmosphere that makes it look that way. Charlie didn't say a word. Apart from Matt's voice, you could only hear the muted whirring of the engine and the pinging noises of rubble flung by the wheels into the undercarriage.

Matt was persistent and explained to Charlie that if you went up above the clouds and out into space, the sunlight would be strong enough to grill you like a chorizo if you didn't have a protective suit on.

# GRANHAMMAR

When he had run out of conversational topics, my brother came down to me in the driver's cab and sank into the passenger seat. With a firm grip on the brace in the ceiling, he tried to do his best to counter the movements of the vehicle as we lurched forward over the rolling ash dunes. His face was pale and he breathed heavily through his nose. He tried to hum a melody but it mostly sounded like a moan.

Matt suffered from motion sickness so he always made sure there were motion sickness bags on these expeditions. But this time he kept it together. I assume he really didn't want to be sick in front of the boy.

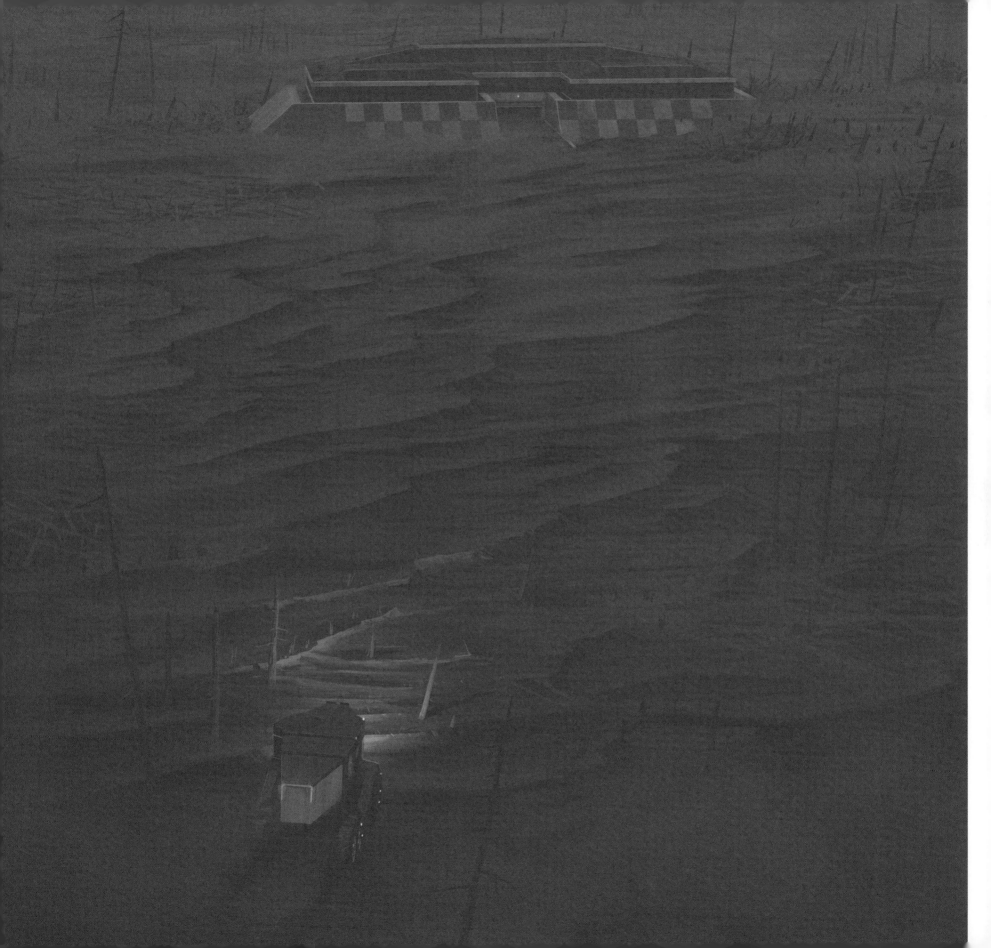

When we arrived, the building had been vacant for several months. A thin covering of soot and other airborne particles had been deposited on the exterior during the winter storms and the ash dunes had started to creep onto the driveway but otherwise the station looked to be in good shape.

Charlie asked about the mural in the garage. Matt said it depicted dandelion seeds blowing in the wind. On the way up to the staff quarters, Matt told Charlie about what troublemakers he and I were when we were young, how we tricked a girl on our street to eat a dandelion so her tongue became completely yellow.

After Matt and I had carried up all the food, the rest of the evening was spent preparing the vehicle for the next day's excursion.

When we finally returned from the garage, Charlie had already gone to bed. He had taken a room with a bunk bed and lay on the top with the tape recorder next to him and his earphones in. That meant he didn't want to be disturbed.

He became like this about a year ago, shortly after he turned thirteen. Went quiet, if you will. And he had always been so chatty. At the same time the problems started at school. The fights.

In my defense, I wasn't the only one who interpreted this as normal adolescent development. Even the psychologist thought that his behavior would improve in his later teens, once his hormones had stabilized.

I woke up early the next day, long before the others. I looked into my brother's room. He was in bed, snoring, curled up on his side with the bedclothes stuffed between his thighs. I studied him for a while, remembering when he used to suck his thumb. He did it far too long. He must have been six when he stopped. He had been afraid of the dark. An open bookcase divided our room in Frödingsvägen and I remember how I would look through it when Mom and Dad sat with him at bedtime – how they tucked him in and whispered soothing things to him until he fell asleep.

I closed the door as quietly as I could and went up to the kitchen. There was half an hour left before the alarm clock was set to ring. I laid down on the kitchen sofa and listened to the various sounds of the station. Far down there in the foundation, the heating system was burning acetyl – the only thing the Black Globes excrete that we have actually found a use for.

At breakfast, it seemed like Charlie was in a pretty good mood. He ate two helpings of sugared corn flakes. Matt was cheerful. He had found an old cassette tape of the Beach Boys that he played in the tape recorder in the kitchen. He stood at the stove and sang along to the music as he prepared deluxe scrambled eggs. With an elegant gesture, he sprinkled basil leaves over the scramble. He spun around and pointed at Charlie with the spatula and said: "You're thinking, 'What kind of strange old music is that?' aren't you?" Then he held the spatula to his phone like a microphone and wailed in a falsetto:

"GOOD GOOD GOOD GOOD VIBRATIONS!"

Honestly speaking, he did get Charlie to smile. A very tiny smile, lightning fast, but it made Matt overjoyed. You could see him having to restrain himself from hugging the boy. When we had eaten, Matt took Charlie around the station and showed him how everything worked: how you used the TV and the microwave, how you logged into the computers in the computer room, how you started the games.

He would manage wonderfully. And if everything went well, we would be back around three o'clock and when we came back, we would all sit down to pork fillets and hasselback potatoes.

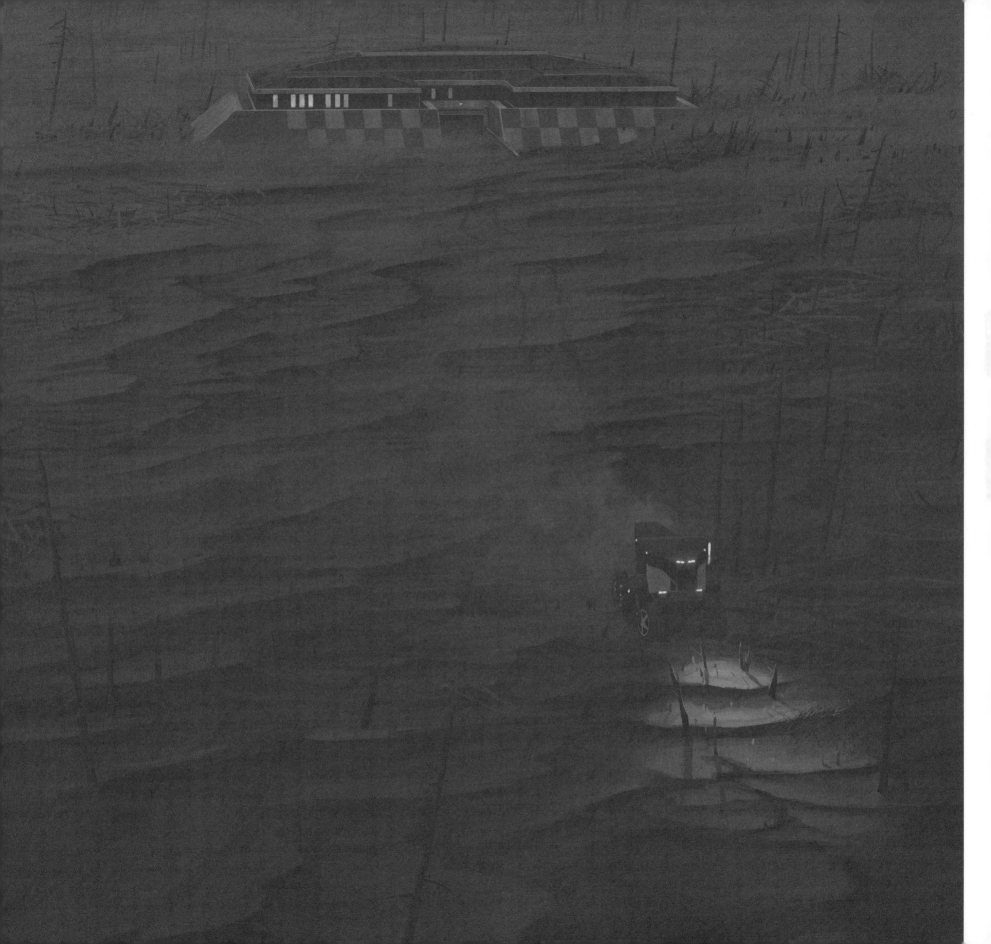

Press any key to continue_

# THE CITY

The first excursion went without a hitch. There had not been any major changes since last year. We focused on the new colonies of Striata that had spread along the smaller roads in the city center. We even took some ash samples and changed out a broken weather sensor.

Matt was in a talkative mood. The new management was apparently incompetent. New routines that in some way made things difficult for the officers, I wasn't really listening. Surface excursions always made him a little nervous. I think it's the suit – he had never liked tight spaces. But he still seemed happy about the progress with Charlie at breakfast. He said several times that he was so happy that Charlie was with us on this expedition.

He babbled on about everything except what we were doing. It was admittedly understandable since Matt on these excursions had no other responsibility than safety and to assist me as needed. But when I was going to take samples of a giant, fragile exuviae, I had to shush him and explain that I needed to concentrate.

We returned to Granhammar at four o'clock, one hour later than planned, mostly because a landslide had made one of the marked roads impassable, forcing us on a long detour to get out of downtown.

When we got back, Charlie was sitting at the computer playing games, just as we left him. He did not answer when we called and did not even seem to have noticed that we were gone. Matt walked over to him and tried to engage in the game for a while but Charlie only answered Matt in monosyllabic mumbles.

I went to the lab for a few hours and sorted the samples from the day's outing and when I came up again, Matt was standing in the kitchen in an apron, preparing dinner. He sliced the pork fillet into pieces and hummed the song from breakfast. When he saw me, he repeated his Beach Boys imitation. I smiled at him. He opened the oven and checked the potatoes, then turned to me, held his finger to his mouth and looked around theatrically. He pulled out a green glass bottle and said:

"What does Mademoiselle Ekdal say about a glass of Cabernet Kungshall?"

While Matt was frying the pork fillet pieces, we drank the wine in our plastic cups and chatted about all manner of things. Matt told me about his new job down in the West City and I complained about the staffing shortages at the hospital.

Suddenly Charlie stood in the doorway. He had something over his head. The kitchen was fairly dark and at first I thought he had his hood pulled up but then I saw from the pattern of the fabric that it was one of the station's pillow cases he had pulled over his head. Both Matt and I became dead quiet. "BOO!" Charlie said behind his pillow case. Matt and I stared at each other. This didn't even happen when he was younger and extroverted.

"Jesus, Charlie! You scared me!" I said, with complete honestly. He shuffled over to me with outstretched arms, moaning. As soon as he was within reach, I grabbed the pillow case and pulled it off. His hair was rumpled and he gave me a strange look. In the dark, I couldn't tell if he was being serious or making a face and that made me even more nervous. I held up my hands like claws and growled at him. Then he just sighed and shuffled out of the kitchen again. I glanced at Matt. He looked terrified.

The following day we walked through a large cluster of albopictus that stretched high toward the dirty sky. With the help of a pipette, I gathered a dark liquid that ran down the stalks. Matt was walking a couple of meters in front of me. He was quiet. I asked him what he was thinking about but he didn't answer. When we were back at the car and I gave him the bag with all the filled test tubes, he looked at me through the visor and said:

"What do you think that pillow case thing was all about?"

"Nothing," I answered. But Matt wasn't satisfied. So this was what he had been thinking about.

"Do you think he was trying to say something? Is he angry at us, do you think?" he went on.

"I don't know, Matt. He's a teenager now. You're angry at everyone at that age."

We didn't talk any more about it that day. When we came back, Matt wanted to show Charlie the samples but he didn't seem interested at all. It's true that the small crumbly samples of Striata husks we had gathered the day before weren't much to look at but not even the colorful Maculatus leaves we had just gathered at Black Island caught his interest, even though Matt did everything he could to try to reach him. He put his arm around the boy and said things like: "this is super rad, check this out" and "you're going to die when you see the thorns on this sucker." I didn't want to stick my nose in and was grateful for the things I had to do in the lab.

The next day, there was a minor incident in the city.

We were gathering samples in the area around one of the old churches. Matt was walking behind me, talking about Charlie. He had a lot of plans for what we were going to do with the boy when we got back to Kungshall. Extra help with his homework of course. It was important that he not fall behind in school. And it was high time the boy started with sports. Some kind of team sport. He needed to learn to become a team player. And also, Matt didn't think the psychologist was so good for him anymore. She just opened a lot of old wounds that needed to heal.

I walked crouched over, filling containers with small outgrowths of what looked like a kind of red parvifolius. Suddenly, I realized that Matt had stopped talking and I turned around. He sat slumped in an ash dune, hanging his head.

I rushed over to him and asked him what had happened. He said he had suddenly started to have palpitations, that he just needed to rest for a while. I immediately started to check his equipment but everything looked as if it was in order. He squeezed his eyes shut for a long time and then he said: "It's so stupid but when I saw that wreck over there, my anxiety came back. Yes, you know. From before." I looked around while at the same time I told him to focus on his

breathing. He stared down at the ash and drew a couple of deep breaths. That's when I saw it.

On a side street in front of us, there was the wreck of a giant armored drone, like the ones the military police used in the crisis years.

Immediately I knew what Matt meant. The memory came back like a film clip. The young men lined up in a row, their heads bent. Still boys, not much older than Charlie. The thrushes that had grown fat on fallen fruit. Was it the last time I saw live birds? The drone that glided majestically and silently behind the island, like an enormous mechanical primeval creature with the police walking in front of it. It was led forward through the wet grass. The muted thuds when it fired. Was it muted because I held my hands over my ears? I wasn't standing very far away. The thrushes scattered at the shots. Bodies were ripped apart, one after the other. Disintegrated. The lower half of a body was thrown violently through the air. The feet lacked shoes, one foot had lost its sock. In the silence afterwards, I met Matt's gaze. Dear God, why hadn't he closed his eyes? Instead, he walked around with that sock for hours afterward. Tried to find its foot.

I turned away from the wreck and walked back to my brother on the ash dune. Sat down beside him, took his hand and squeezed it as hard as I could through the glove. We sat like that for a long time.

Later that night, I was woken up by Matt passing by out in the corridor. I knew from the steps that it was him. I listened. The toilets were next door to my room and I could clearly hear him run the water in one of the sinks in there. He let it run for a long time. When he finally turned off the tap, I could hear a faint mumbling, as if he was talking to someone. I couldn't discern any words through the wall but he sounded upset. Was he talking in his sleep? I gently pressed my ear to the woven wallpaper. Now I could almost hear the words. After a while, I realized that he was repeating the same phrase over and over, and soon I also understood what he was saying. He said it quietly, almost as a whisper, and there was a desperate rage in how he spit out the words: "… they were planning to kill us all… they didn't give us a choice."

The following morning, I went in to try and wake Charlie but he refused to get up or get out of bed. I didn't have the energy to argue so I walked out to the kitchen. Matt was there, looking out the window. When I entered the room, he said, without turning around: "Good morning, my dear" in an exaggerated British accent and asked if I had slept well. He misunderstood what I answered and said "How wonderful!" I took breakfast supplies out of the refrigerator, sat down at the kitchen table and started to make a sandwich.

"Do you see anything?" I asked and took a bite of my sandwich. Matt did not react for a long time but finally he turned to me. He looked pale and sickly, as if he had not gotten any sleep all night. He sat down and poured out milk and oat cereal in a bowl. Then he said: "Dust whirls."

After breakfast, we made our final excursion. Matt was distant and quiet all day. He had clearly slept very little but there was something else as well. When we packed the last samples into the car, he over-turned a rack of test tubes.

On the way back, I tried to chat a little but he just sat there with an empty gaze. When we finally arrived back at Granhammar and I turned off the engine in the garage, he suddenly grabbed my shoulder.

"He stood by my bed last night," he said. "Just like in the kitchen. With the pillow case over his head."

We ate dinner in silence and afterward, when Charlie disappeared into his computer, Matt said:

"We have to talk to him, Sigrid. I can't take this anymore."

I started to clear the dishes and said: "It'll be fine when he gets back to his friends in school." Even though both Matt and I knew he didn't have any friends anymore. Matt sighed and said: "I think he is starting to remember. The pillow case, Sigrid. Isn't it obvious?"

I didn't answer and instead went up to the counter and rinsed the plates. Matt sat hunched over with his head in his hands. When I was going to wipe off the table he took hold of my wrist and said: "Please, Sigrid, listen to me. I really want a chance to explain. I'm sure he would understand if I talked to him. Don't you think it would be good for him? The sacks…" He interrupted himself with a feeble whimper, putting both hands over his mouth and trying to suppress his sobs.

I sat down next to him and wrapped my arms around him, kissing him on the forehead and telling him that everything would be alright. Then I sang a lullaby that Dad used to sing for us when we were little. I couldn't remember the words but hummed the melody and felt Matt slowly relax in my arms.

I had been sitting in the lab for hours. I got nothing done, just sat and stared at the samples. Matt's words lingered, they settled like a hard clump in my stomach. Everything was starting to fall apart.

For some reason, I started to think of the little house we would go to in the summers when Matt and I were little. We had a problem with ants. I remember lying on the lacquered wooden floor, staring at the motorway that the ants had created between the veranda and the kitchen. Dad placed out small round plastic cases filled with ant poison. Because you don't kill the ants one by one. All you have to do is infect a couple of them who then bring the poison to the rest of the colony. You let the ants exterminate themselves. It takes a while. You have to be patient. But one day, they are all dead or dying, small black crumbs on the floor of the house. The ants themselves will never understand what happened.

The thought of the dead ants made my intestines contract. I shut my eyes but could only see bodies dissolving. In any case – that was when the power went out.

There was a powerful explosion somewhere in the station, followed by total darkness.

These stations remind me of passenger planes. The similarities are striking now that I think back on it. In the airplane, everything was constructed in order to distract passengers from the fact that they were sitting a couple of centimeters from an environment entirely lethal to the human body. That's why airplanes were full of comforting objects from life on the ground. Lifestyle magazines, food and alcohol. I once flew with a carrier that had received a prize for its wine cellar.

The last seven years, I had allowed myself to be lulled into a similar sense of security. And when the power went out at Granhammar, I suddenly became aware of our actual situation, just like passengers in an airplane at 10,000 meters when the engines have just failed. No parachutes but a mature Bordeaux.

The power outage only lasted for a few seconds, then the diesel generator started and the emergency lighting came on. My first thought was that Charlie must be terrified, so I rushed up the four floors to the staff quarters but I could not find either Charlie or Matt. The common room was empty and lit by a dim red glow. The TV and videoplayer had been reset by the power going out and on the screen, there was a message floating around that read "NO SIGNAL." The kitchen, where I had left Matt, was also empty as were the bedrooms. I walked over to the computer room where I assumed Charlie had been when the power went out. but the computer room was empty. Charlie's computer was on and there was something on the screen, so I stepped closer to read what it was.

It was self-evident. His introversion, the outbursts, the fights at school – none of it had anything to do with hormones. This was not a case of adolescent troubles. And the pillow cases, dear God. Matt had been right the whole time. Charlie knew.

C:\>i know whats in the bags
Bad command or file name

C:\>the bags
Bad command or file name

C:\>i know what you put there
Bad command or file name

C:\>i know whats in the bag i knwo whats in the bag inside the bag
                    qwhats inside      i know i know i know i know whats in the ba
Bad command or file name

C:\> i know whats in the bag i know i know i know i know i know i know
                                              i know I KNOW WHATS INSIDE



Bad command or file name

C:\>

                                        WHATS IN THE BAG I KNOW

Some may pretend not to know or that they have forgotten. Just like me and Matt. But we all knew what was in those sacks. We know very well that it is thanks to their contents that we can live our comfortable lives down here in Kungshall.

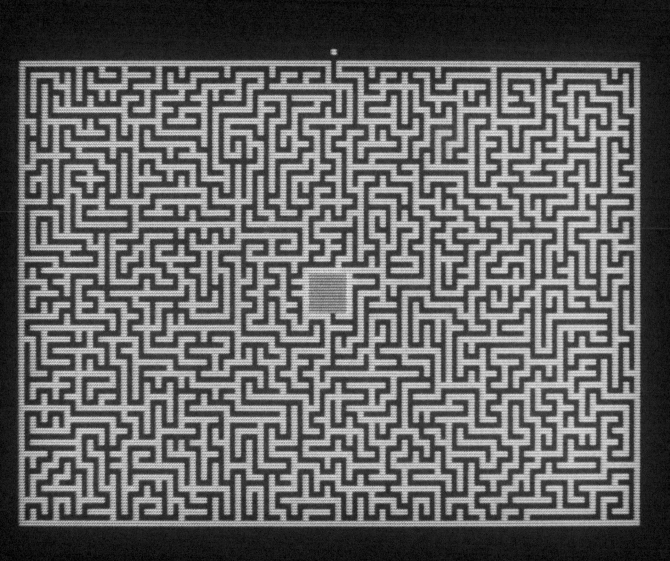

# CHARLIE

No one can say who his real parents were. But we know that Charlie had a big brother called Alex. We often talked about him in the beginning. The psychologist said it was good for Charlie. "When will Alex get here?" he would ask. We told him that he had run away and that he wouldn't come back. We wanted to tell him what really happened. We were going to tell him the whole truth – that Alex was dead – but in some way it just never happened. Time went by and eventually Charlie stopped asking about Alex. We never talked about it with each other but I assume we hoped that he had forgotten. That he had repressed his memories of his time before Kungshall.

Yes, the time before Kungshall – how will we ever be able to talk about it?

The black globes had been pumping their toxins into our atmosphere for over a decade. People were sick and dying. Chaos was about to break out. In hindsight it feels like everything went very quickly, from one day to another, but I remember that I was restless, in a constant state of frustration that nothing was happening. I belonged to the research community and we realized that if no drastic measures were taken that humanity would become extinct. It was painful to have to see the world collapse as the politicians and the public spent all their time trying to assign blame to someone.

When my brother told me about the Kungshall project, I felt an indescribable relief. A project for our survival was being sketched out and I was needed. His friends within the military were willing to hire me on the spot simply because I was a doctor. And when Kungshall was finished they would likely need my expertise in microbiology.

We were asked to construct a completely new, hermetically sealed society – a subterranean city with room for 100,000 inhabitants. We would do this as the old society was collapsing violently around us.

By this point, the atmosphere was noticeably difficult to breathe. Europe was breaking down into lawlessness. Unknown illnesses were spreading uncontrollably among the fleeing masses. There was total panic and desperation among the refugees. Rumors of Kungshall and where it was located passed among the hundreds of thousands of people who were constantly streaming up from the south. Cities were plundered and burned down in indiscriminate hatred. Violent groups joined forces in what started to resemble an open war against the military. In us they found a mutual enemy. We knew that they had acquired powerful weapons. There were even rumors that they had obtained a new kind of biological agent. That was what we were most afraid of – that an infection would spread down in Kungshall. And the responsibility lay with us to make sure that something like that would never happen.

Violence was everywhere. Also on our side. It can't be denied that we never would have managed to complete the project without violence.

One has to keep in mind that Kungshall was never intended to function as a shelter where you could squeeze in as many needy as possible. It was a carefully constructed independent life supporting system completely separate from the surface of the Earth. Each selected person with their individual skills and needs was accounted for in the calculation. The system would manage to keep its inhabitants alive for generations if needed. There were detailed plans in place for the gene pool of the entire population. There was simply no longer any space to worry about how people up there were being treated. What should we have done? A priority-based system where the most desperate were given shelter? Everyone was desperate.

A quarantine zone was erected. We swept through the zone like a giant search party hunting for trespassers. The fields were mined. Heavily armed robots patrolled the border. No one would be able to pass. When the doors to Kungshall were closed for the last time, we needed to be sure that the surface above it was secured. All possible threats to the project were annihilated.

The strategy was simple: deterrence. The methods grew from the bottom up, from the field patrols of the military police. We had no name for it but one wasn't needed. We never spoke of it.

The important thing was that it worked. The streams of refugees diminished. The violence and attacks abated. The message had been received: *whatever misery you are fleeing from, something much worse awaits you here.*

That summer, the trees never bloomed. The black globes had thickened the atmosphere to the point that what little sunlight reached the surface was not enough. The vegetation lay diseased and thickened in the ditches. It was a new kind of autumn, a long and drawn-out season of illness and death that would soon give way to an eternal, pitch black winter. The water in the ground was starting to freeze and soon a sooty snow would begin to fall. I remember that it was all so still. The screams had stopped and in the new silence there was a kind of peace.

We had started to relax. Fear slowly started to loosen its grip on us. Now the work was almost over and we would finally have the chance to rest in safety down in Kungshall's newly built and warm spaces. Many people removed their helmets and talked. Some walked around, taking in the landscape. They knew they would never see it again. Some cried.

I remember the final weeks as very peaceful. We clearly saw many things that were frightening but a kind of calm lay over everything, the knowledge that it was over. The horrors had stopped affecting me anyway, my brain had grown used to them.

In a ditch, there was part of a lower body, belonging to a young woman. White thighs gleamed in the dead grass, the skin peeled back like a soft husk where the body had been pierced by the bullets of the military police. I remember it was there and then I realized that my instinct to avert my gaze had disappeared. It was what it was. And it was over. The suffering was over. The only feeling in me was that of relief.

One day, we seized a young man who was passing through the quarantine zone. He was in his late teens, maybe eighteen. Definitely not yet twenty. He had his little brother with him. He was wearing a jacket with a red mark on the back: a red ringed fist. It was the symbol of Terra Proxima, one of the armed groups that wanted to overthrow Kungshall. Matt was going to have to walk him over to the field hospital where the Operational Division conducted its interrogations. We both knew what that meant. Matt asked me to stay with the boy in the meantime.

I understood those young people completely. If things had been different, I would maybe even have stood on their side in their fight against the military. Under normal circumstances, that would have been the most humane thing to do.

But I can also understand data. That is my job. And the data was clear: the black globes were exterminating all life on Earth. In order to save humanity, we were forced to be inhumane for a limited period of time. Close down half of ourselves. Kungshall is an enormous freezer where half of the people work on keeping society frozen for when the immediately life-threatening situation on the Earth's surface disappears. There was never any alternative.

We did what was demanded of us. But however well we understood the utility of what we did, our souls were damaged. It is therefore vital to be able to protect one's soul and for that, strength is needed. I am stronger than Matt, you see, I always have been. I have been able to keep the pain away, prevent it from destroying vital organs. It is as if I shrink the pupil of my soul and in this way prevent its inside from burning up. Matt lacks this ability.

When he returned after the interrogation of the teenager, I saw that something in his gaze had changed. Something in his soul had been broken. He just sat quietly in his tent in the base camp for several hours. Finally, he emerged and went straight to the officers' quarters where he remained for a long time. When he came back, he said to me:

"We are allowed to take the boy with us."

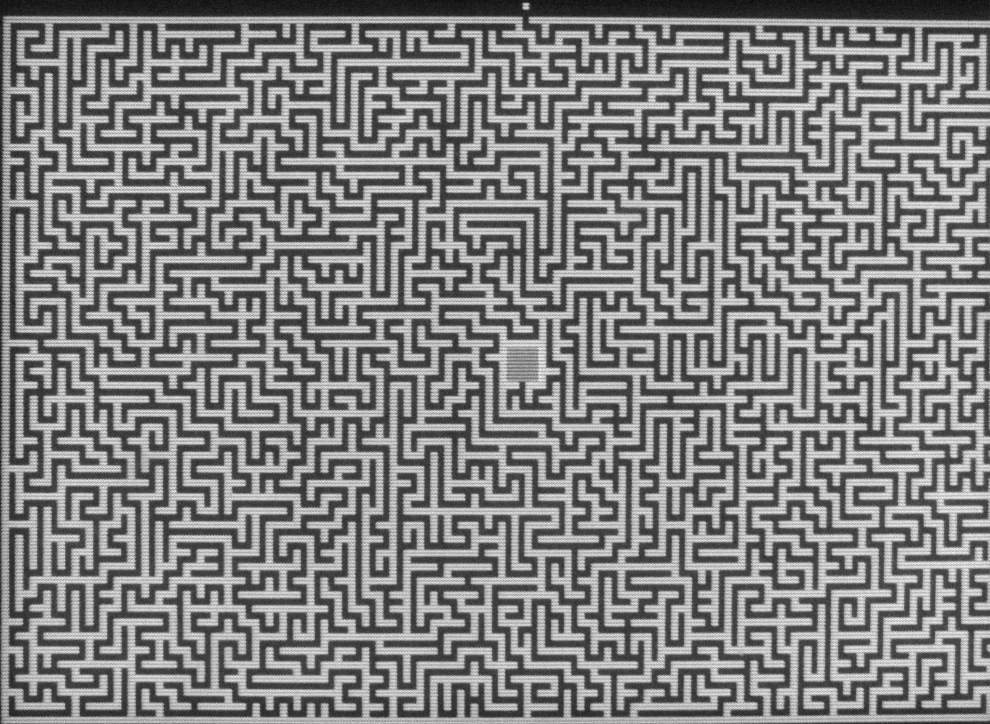

# THE BLACK WATER

You allow the ants to exterminate themselves. They fill their bellies with the poisoned honey and then contentedly set off to the ant colony where they infect every other ant they come into contact with.

It must have happened at that moment, when I found the computer. I called out both their names but they didn't answer.

I assume that Matt's first thought after the power outage was to go to Charlie. And, just as I did, Matt must have found the message on the computer screen.

Did he try to talk to Charlie about it? About what those sacks had contained?

I assume he did his best to get him to understand but did Matt ever have a chance? I mean, to get Charlie to understand? Do we even understand it ourselves? What we did wasn't right. But just because an action is wrong doesn't mean that you can refrain from carrying it out. Not if it is the only option that remains.

Not if there is no other way out.

You can ask for forgiveness afterward. That is all. Was it forgiveness Matt asked for when he found Charlie in that room? I assume so.

But forgiveness isn't necessary. We did what needed to be done, just like the slow-worm. Matt never could understand the business with the slow-worm.

Some things can never be fixed and the question he should have asked himself before entering that room with Charlie is: *can we ever be forgiven for the crimes of which we are guilty?*

I don't think so.

I have thought a lot about what happened that afternoon seven years ago. I should never have allowed the boy to walk around the camp. Matt had told me to take care of the boy and I thought I had him in my sight the whole time. But in some way Charlie must still have seen what we had done with his brother.

In the end, he must have understood what was in the sacks and he wanted to make it clear to me that he knew. In a way we are even now. We took his brother and he took mine.

Bad command or file name

C:\>

Quit to DOS? (Y/N)_

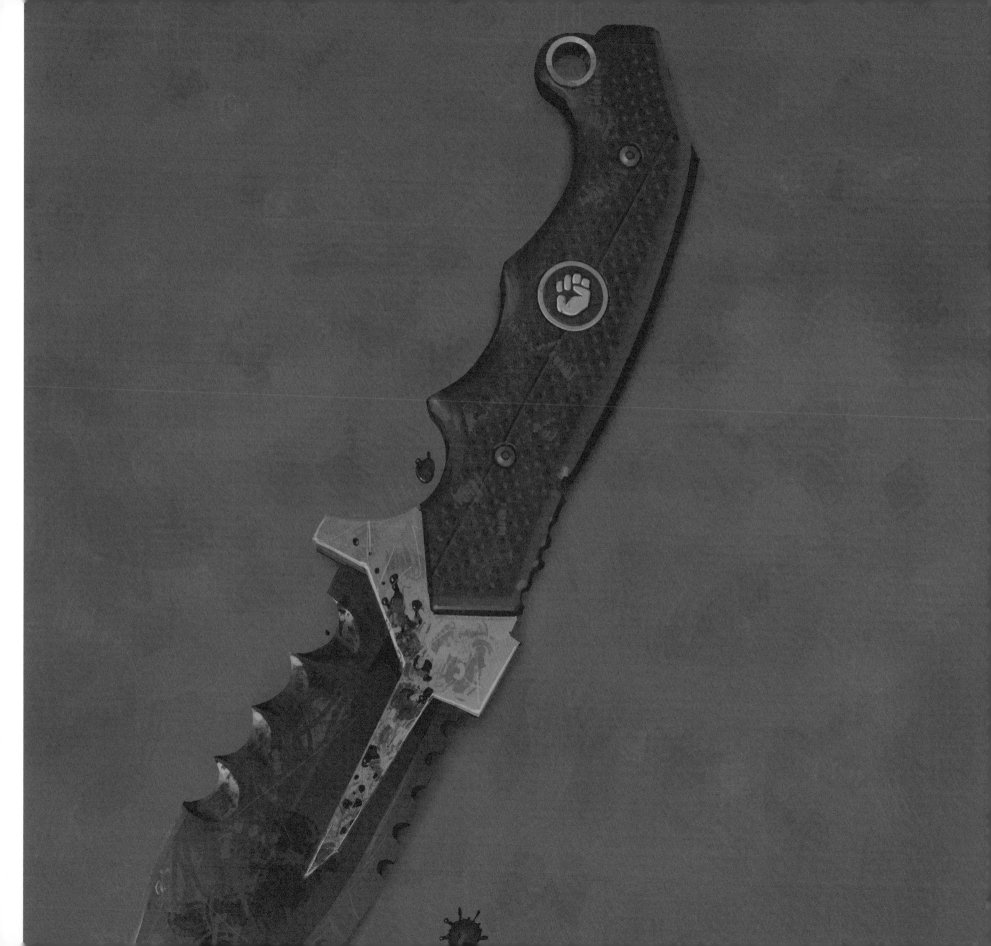

Matt wanted to buy himself free by taking care of the child. He thought you could repay a debt in that way. And I wanted to buy myself free by allowing Matt this self-deception. But I should have said no back then, seven years ago. I was maybe stronger than my brother but I wasn't strong enough to say no to him.

It's kind of funny when you think about it. We never checked the tape recorder. I have trouble believing that the military police would have let a tape recorder slip by into Kungshall. It must have been Matt who got it through the check points. His guilty conscience. He had taken the little boy's brother, he couldn't make himself take the tape recorder as well.

How long had Charlie known? For seven years, the knife was taped to the inside of the tape recorder. Did he wait until we were alone at Granhammar or was it the solitude of Granhammar that made him remember? In any case, he did remember and my brother had to pay with his life. I should have realized from the beginning that this catastrophe would catch up with me in the end.

When I stood there by my brother's body, the water arrived. It welled up from the interior of the station. The cold red corridors were filling up with water and then I did what I should have done that afternoon seven years ago. I abandoned the boy.

We must have made errors in our calculations, something regarding the proportions of water and ammonia. The increased pressure in the atmosphere must have meant that the ammonia finally fell like rain and dissolved the frozen water under the ash. I assume they are working intensely on this now. Regardless of what had caused it, the landscape outside the station was now in a state of dissolution. I tried to get away but the all-terrain vehicle was caught up and carried away by the masses of water.

I was sure it was over. For two days, I was stuck in the vehicle. Water had made its way up into the lookout where I had curled up inside my protective suit. I waited for the electricity in the car to go out. Then I would freeze to death. I almost meant to make sure this happened – the thought of filling my lungs with below zero-degree ammonia-water frightened me more than dying of cold. Then I noticed the medical kit on the wall next to me in the lookout. I took it down from the wall and opened it. Small green packages of medicine were neatly packed inside. I lifted a package of gauze and there next to the small ampules of morphine was what I was looking for: a small tin of green metal. I coaxed it out and emptied the contents into the palm of my hand. I had to strain to see them in the dark: four blue capsules, small as grains of rice.

That was when they found me.

They never checked my mouth. How could they forget to do that? That was yet another crack in the security here. All expeditions are furnished with advanced medical equipment and a large supply of medications – everything from paracetamol to morphine. But also these blue capsules with cyanide, four in each medical kit. A legacy of the military, I suppose. Hopefully they will improve their routines after this.

I'm not feeling very well. The capsule must have started to leak. Each time they move me, I have had it in my mouth. I guess it is time to crack it open now. It's not that I'm afraid of the hanging – they are very effective and you die almost immediately. Statistically speaking, it is probably more reliable than biting down on the capsule that I keep moving around in my mouth. But I think I can't handle the thought of someone else doing it. An instinct, simply. Like that of the slow-worm.

I saw something when I was stuck in the vehicle. Or was it a dream? I don't know. But in any case, I saw something. Outside the window, out in the rain, in the mud. A person, a boy. I think it was Charlie. He was walking through the mud. It must have been a dream. Well, obviously, how silly of me, of course it was. I just feel so sleepy. It is so still here now.

## ALSO BY SIMON STÅLENHAG

*Tales from the Loop*
*Things from the Flood*
*The Electric State*

SIMON &
SCHUSTER

First published in Great Britain by Simon & Schuster UK Ltd, 2021

1 3 5 7 9 10 8 6 4 2

Simon & Schuster UK Ltd
1st Floor
222 Gray's Inn Road
London WC1X 8HB

Simon & Schuster Australia, Sydney

Simon & Schuster India, New Delhi

www.simonandschuster.co.uk
www.simonandschuster.com.au
www.simonandschuster.co.in

A CIP catalogue record for this book is available from the British Library

Hardback ISBN: 978-1-3985-0999-3

**Manufactured in Italy**

KUNGSHALL